I0525974

THE WARRIOR AND THE STAR

MARGOT EATON

Copyright © 2025 by Margot Eaton

All rights reserved.

No part of this book may be reproduced in any form or by any electronic or mechanical means, including information storage and retrieval systems, without written permission from the author, except for the use of brief quotations in a book review.

This is a work of fiction. Names, characters, places, and incidents are either the product of the author's imagination or are used fictitiously. Any resemblance to actual persons, living or dead, events, or locales is entirely coincidental.

ISBN: 979-8-9988909-1-8

For Wyatt,
My North Star.
You are the quiet miracle this story was always leading toward.
The heartbeat beneath every sentence.
You were born with a light the world doesn't always understand—
but always feels.
My greatest honor in this life—
is to be your mother.
May you always, always remember:
You can protect your heart without dimming your light.

All you have to do is believe.
  And the current will meet you.
  — Sage

CONTENTS

The Stars Are Listening

For those who have ever whispered to the stars,
wondering if anyone was listening—
they were.
You are not alone.
You are not lost.
You are becoming.

— Margot Eaton

I F YOU'RE HOLDING THIS BOOK, THE STAR HAS SOMETHING TO SAY TO YOU...

HAVE YOU EVER WONDERED WHAT HAPPENS WHEN YOU WISH UPON A STAR?

I HEARD YOU.

LONG BEFORE YOU SPOKE IT.

BEFORE THE WORDS WERE READY,

BEFORE YOU KNEW WHAT TO ASK FOR——

I FELT THE SHAPE OF YOUR LONGING RISE THROUGH THE DARK.

YOU MAY HAVE THOUGHT IT WAS LOST.

THAT IT VANISHED INTO THE SKY.

BUT WISHES DON'T DISAPPEAR.

THEY WAIT.

AND YES... I GRANT THEM.

BUT NOT ALL AT ONCE.

NOT IN THE WAY YOU MIGHT EXPECT.

SOME WISHES ARRIVE WRAPPED IN SILENCE.

SOME REQUIRE YOU TO CLIMB.

SOME COME AS QUESTIONS THAT ECHO UNTIL YOU REMEMBER THE ANSWER WAS ALWAYS INSIDE YOU.

THIS IS ONE OF THOSE WISHES.

A STORY BORN FROM GRIEF,

FROM LIGHT BURIED DEEP BENEATH THE WEIGHT OF FORGETTING.

IT WAITED LIFETIMES FOR SOMEONE LIKE YOU TO FIND IT.

BECAUSE SOMETHING IN YOU STILL BELIEVES.

AND THAT BELIEF...

IT MOVES THINGS.

IT BROUGHT YOU HERE.

TO THIS PAGE.

TO THIS REMEMBERING.

THIS STORY IS NOT JUST A TALE.

IT'S A DOOR.

AND I——

I HAVE BEEN WAITING ON THE OTHER SIDE,
READY TO OPEN.

-THE STAR

Chapter One: The Girl Who Spoke to Stars

The village whispered her name like a curse.

"Myla," they muttered behind closed shutters and narrow glances.

The girl who talks to the stars,

They said it was a shame—

such a strange girl,

born of good people.

She hadn't asked for the gift that set her apart.

Only for someone to stay.

Her mother had left when she was still small—

not in anger,
but because she didn't know how to love a child who looked to
the stars instead of her.
Her real father left soon after.
But not long after,
Jax came into her life—
not by birthright,
but by choice.
And Abuela was already there,
arms open,
as if she'd been waiting all along.
They didn't try to fix her.
They didn't ask her to change.
They just stepped in—quietly, steadily
and became her world.

Abuela cooked warm meals,
    told stories from her childhood,
    and made space for her to simply be.
    She never asked Myla to explain herself.
    She just held her,
    and in the quiet, Myla felt safe.
    Sometimes, while braiding Myla's hair,
    Abuela would say,
    "Mi tesoro, you have your mother's hands—your eyes, they're
mine."
    Then they'd giggle, and Myla would rest against her,
    Abuela would kiss her softly on her forehead.
    In her arms, Myla felt loved.
    Safe.

Jax's love came in quiet acts of teaching and protection.

He taught her how to walk the forest trails without getting lost,
how to read the sky for signs of rain,
which berries were safe,
where wild mint grew,
how to build a fire that didn't smoke,
and how to climb the mountain
and move through the woods as if she always belonged there.

When the other children left her out,
    Jax would lift her onto his shoulders and say,
    "You're not missing anything down there.
    Look up.
    That's where you belong."
    And when she cried,
    doubting her place in the world,
    he'd hold her close and whisper,
    "I'll always be there for you. You know that."
    She believed him.
    She still did.

Even now,
    with both of them returned to the sky,
    shining from somewhere just beyond the veil—
    she felt Jax in the wind.
    In the way the stars brightened.
    In the silence between her thoughts.
    He was still with her.
    Watching.
    Walking beside her.

But the village had never seen that side of her life.

When the villagers spoke,
she didn't always know what to say.
Sometimes, the words just didn't come.
They pushed her away with silence,
with doors that didn't open,
and eyes that slid past her as if she wasn't there.
She learned to stay quiet.
To sit in corners.
To breathe slowly until the world softened again.

She remembered the first time someone looked at her as though she
didn't belong—
    She had only been six.
    A boy at the village well had asked her a question—
    but she'd been listening to the wind.
    When she took too long to find the words,
    He made a face.
    "You're not like us," he said, backing away.
    Myla had wanted to explain.
    But there was nothing to say.
    She'd been listening to something only she could hear.

After Abuela's presence became a memory,
    the house grew quiet again.
    But this time,
    no one knocked.
    No one asked if she was alright.
    Maybe they thought she'd manage.
    Maybe they thought she was old enough to feed herself.

At first, she waited—
for someone to notice.
For someone to care.
But no one came.
So she found quiet ways to comfort herself.
She would place her right hand on her heart,
and rest her left hand softly against her cheek,
tilting her head into it—
as if borrowing the warmth she wished someone else would
offer.

She hummed slow, gentle notes to soothe the silence.
She whispered stories under her breath,
the kind Abuela used to tell.
And when the ache grew too heavy,
she'd close her eyes and say,
"It's okay. I'm here."
And somehow... that helped.
She didn't remember when the whispers began.
Only that once they did,
they never stopped.

She was too strange to be kept close,
too quiet to be missed.

Someone once said, "She's nearly grown,"
    not to her—
    but near enough that she heard it.
    As if that meant she didn't need comfort.
    Company.
    Or anyone at all.
    But Myla didn't hear them anymore.
    She stopped trying to fix what wasn't broken.
    She started listening to the parts of the world
    that made sense to her.
    She stopped listening to people—
    and started listening to the wind.
    To the stars.
    The ones that never left.

She remembered being someone's granddaughter.
    Someone's daughter.
    Remembered being wrapped in abuela's quilts,
    smelling of clove tea and earth.
    Being kissed gently on the forehead.
    Being told bedtime stories of star maidens and soulfire.
    She remembered a voice that never rushed her.
    Hands that steadied her steps.
    A gaze that never asked her to be anything but herself.

The village had forgotten the stars—
    forgotten they were ever connected to them.
    But Myla hadn't.

She loved them all.
The bright ones that sparkled like laughter.
The ones that blinked in patterns only she could see.
The ones that glided across the sky like silver ribbons.
She made little wishes.
Quiet ones.

But one night,
she made a different kind of wish.
A wish for love.
For someone to see her.
To sit beside her without asking her to change.
For a voice that said, *I love you exactly as you are.*
The stars did not answer—not at first.
But then, one night, one of them did.
It glowed differently than the rest—dimly flickering,
not a light,
but like a heartbeat.
It was struggling to shine.
This was no ordinary star.
It pulsed with something ancient,
something aching.
And when the wind fell still,
and the world held its breath,
the star spoke without sound:

I need you, Warrior.
  Come find me.
  I cannot shine without you.

She told the villagers what she heard.

They said she was cursed.
Possessed.
Cracked open by grief and clinging to ghosts.
When she pointed to the sky and said, "It's speaking to me,"
the elders gathered beneath the fading light of a full moon.
They called her a danger.
A threat to their peace.
They had long abandoned the stars—
forgotten the sky was once a mirror,
not a mystery.
They feared what reminded them of their own forgetting.
And so they cast it out.
Because it is easier to exile the light
than to face the darkness it reveals.
They exiled her to the forest.
To the edge of the known.
To the mountain.

The mountain wasn't unfamiliar.
    Jax had shown her the trails long ago—
    how to climb without slipping,
    how to take in thinner air,
    how to trust her footing
    and even now, as the villagers turned away—
    she felt the sting of being cast out.
    But somewhere inside, a voice said,
    It's alright.
    Let them turn away.
    This mountain was Jax's.
    And if no one else will have me–
    Jax's mountain will.

· · ·

No one stopped her as she left.

No one called her back.

No one asked where she would go.

She looked back once.

But there was no one left to wave her home.

She thought of Jax then.

And Abuela.

And the way their love had never asked her to be anyone other than herself.

She was only a child.

But she did not scream.

She did not plead.

She turned her gaze upward.

And whispered,

"I'm coming."

The star was calling.

And she had always known:

It would never stop.

And maybe what came next

would break her.

Or build her.

Or both.

But whatever it was—

it would be shaped by her hands.

And so she stepped forward—

not to escape the past,

but to answer the call.

The one that flickered faintly above her—

dim, pulsing, waiting.

Chapter Two: The Path Beyond the Gate

The forest waited in silence.
　　It was the kind of silence that didn't feel empty,
　　but full—
　　as if something was listening.
　　Myla stood just beyond the village's outer stone gate,
　　where the lanterns stopped burning
　　and the dirt turned to root—wound path.
　　Her satchel was light.
　　Her heart, heavy.
　　She didn't look back.

But she thought about it.

She thought about her abuela's house—quiet but warm
    The spot by the window looking up at the stars—
    where she and Abuela would nestle under layered blankets
    stitched with stories only they remembered.
    Safe and familiar.
    She thought of the silence after they were gone.

    The villagers.

    The way they had turned their faces from her as if she was wind-
blown ash.
    The way no one knocked.
     No one called her name.
    Still, her feet hesitated.
    She asked herself
    What if the star was just a dream?
    What if this path led to nowhere?
    What if I could not save the star?
    What if I failed?
    She gripped the strap of her satchel tighter.
    A knot rising in her throat.
    What if this was a trick of the mind?
    A wave of air curled around her back
    guiding her forward,
    Not impatient, but encouraging.
    as if even the trees had grown weary of waiting for her to begin.
    She stepped past the last boundary she had ever known.

The world changed.
    The air turned colder, cleaner.

Leaves glistened with dew.
Every sound was louder–
her own footsteps,
the fluttering of wings overhead,
the slow inhale of the earth.
She walked.
For how long, she didn't know.
Time lost its rhythm in the wild.
There were no bells here.
No rituals.
No judgment.
Just sky, soil and space.
The sun was warm on her shoulders.
The trees swayed gently.
A bird sang.
But it all felt a world away—
Her mind was loud.
Her body, heavy.
The ache in her chest drowned out the wind.
It wasn't just the walking,
or the weight of her satchel.
It was the wound of being sent away—
as if she were something to fear,
Something to forget.
Her very existence had been too much to bear.
She hadn't just been cast out.
Unwanted.
Unclaimed.

But with every step,
the forest began to speak.
Not in words, but in feeling—
a stillness in the air,

the sheen of morning dew on leaves,
the pulse beneath the soil—
and slowly, rain sinking into dry earth,
life began to reach her.
Not in sound,
but in the soft hush of shifting leaves,
where the earth speaks softly to those who've forgotten,
and teaches them how to feel again,
it began to find its way back in.
Not all at once,
but in breaths and sacred silence,
Until her heart remembered how to listen to nature's quiet voice.

She began to hum,
    soft at first.
    Then she heard a nearby bird—clear and curious—
    Call out: Ti—ree? Tir—ree?
    She mimicked the sound,
    Tilting her head to catch the rhythm.
    Again and again,
    she repeated the melody,
    carrying it with her
    through the forest to greet the mountain.
    Each echo smoothed the restless places inside her.

She paused and pulled her coat tighter.
    It had been Abuela's.
    Not just sewn by her—but worn by her.
    The deep blue wool still carried the scent of clove, cinnamon and
earth,
    and across the back and sleeves,
    stars twinkled—

stitched in gold thread by Abuela's own hands.
The sleeves fell past her wrists,
and when she walked,
her hem brushed the tops of her boots.
It didn't quite fit right.
But that was okay.
It was wearing a piece of the night sky—
the same sky Abuela used to tell stories about,
where wishes lived.
Wrapped in that memory, Myla felt braver.
As if each star sewn into the fabric was a promise:
You are not alone.
And so, she kept walking.
The trees thinned, and the sky opened.
That's when she saw it.

. . .

The mountain.

It stood with a quiet strength—
    ancient, unmoving, alive.
    Not demanding her attention.
    Just... allowing her to arrive.
    There was something about it—
    the shape of it,
    the silence of it,
    that made her feel she was home.
    Not the kind with walls or people.
    The kind you carry inside.
    Not even Abuela's warm kitchen
    nor the comfort of her blankets
    had felt quite like home.
    Because even there, she had still been alone.

But this mountain...
    This was his mountain.
    Jax had taught her its secrets.
    How to move through it without disturbing it.
    How to find food and fire without fear.
    How to survive—
    not by conquering the wild,
    but by becoming part of it.
    He hadn't just taught her how to live out here.
    He'd taught her how to belong to something that didn't ask her
to be different.
    And standing there now,
    she realized something:

This was the only place she had ever truly been herself.
The only place that didn't ask her to explain, shrink, or prove.
The mountain gave her what the village never could:
A place to just... "be."

So she stepped forward.
The path began to rise beneath her feet—
slow at first,
as though the mountain honored her first steps.
She didn't rush.
She didn't look back.
She told herself,
This is it.
The beginning.
She climbed through dusk,
She rested on a rock near a moss-covered tree
and took out a small cloth bundle from her satchel.
Inside was her Abuela's necklace,
a gold charm shaped like a spiral galaxy.
Myla pressed it to her chest and placed it beside her on the rock.
Then she gathered a few twigs and
crouched beside a patch of earth darkened by dew.

The sun was beginning to sink,
casting long fingers of gold through the trees.
Myla glanced at the sky—
she didn't have much daylight left.
She pulled out her bundle of twigs and crouched near a patch of
damp earth, trying to remember Jax's voice.
"Small teepee.
Dry kindling.
Airflow, Myla.

Just breathe."
But the spark wouldn't catch.
The sunlight was fading.
Her patience thinned along with the sky.
She struck the flint once.
Nothing.
Just a dull spark, swallowed by dampness.
Again.
Still nothing.
The wind changed direction.
Her fingers numbed.
The sky dimmed, and her spirit dimmed with it.
She struck harder this time,
but her hand slipped, scraping her knuckle.
She gasped and dropped the flint.
Frustration surged.
She stood too quickly, brushing off her cloak with shaking
hands—
and her foot caught a root hidden behind leaves.
The ground tilted.
She stumbled forward,
arms flailing, and landed hard on her side.
A low branch snapped across her shoulder,
and a sharp sting bloomed where she hit the earth.
Leaves quivered around her.
Her satchel slipped from her shoulder.
And for a moment, she just lay there.
Then—
She slammed her fist into the ground.
Dirt scattered beneath her fingers.
She pushed herself up,
brushing moss from her hair
and blinking back tears.
She tilted her head back,

feet stomping on the ground
with both arms reaching up and yelled at the sky:

"This shouldn't be so hard!"

Her voice came sharp and trembling at the edges.
Her knuckle throbbed, and her chest ached in that hollow
echoing way only deep missing can cause.
Jax had taught her this and so much more.
Not just how to make a fire.
He'd made it fun—
She'd watch him work,
whistling and naming each stick as if they were royalty—
Sir Crackle, Lady Tinder, and with a bow, Mr. Twiggles himself.
She used to giggle until she couldn't breathe.

Then came the flood—
    joy, longing, rejection, warmth, the sharp edge of abandonment,
    the ache of being seen once and now being unseen.
    She felt small.
    Remembered how big Jax's hands had been.
    How safe they made her feel.
    She felt everything, all at once.
    Grief and love,
    fear and memory,
    rejection
    and safety.
    It surged through her body, too much for one moment to hold.
    And so, with every emotion pressing at once—
    She exhaled into the dark, "I'm scared, Jax."
    Her voice barely rose above a breath.
    "I'm scared", she said again,
    the words broken on trembling lips,

 barely holding together.
"Was I lying to myself? she muttered.
When I thought I could do this without you?"
She looked at her scraped knuckle.
"I miss you" she said, to the trees, to the wind, to the sky.
"This is harder without you..."
"But I'm still here.
I'm still trying.
Can you see me?
Hear me?"
A hush moved through the branches above her
and brushed her cheek.
She took a pause,
gathered the driest twigs she could find,
and tried again—
quieter this time,
with presence and calm.
She envisioned the flame more reverently–
And this time the flame caught.
Small at first,
trembling,
unsure
But real.
She summoned the spark,
with tender hands,
placing the twigs—
a sacred gift into the fire.
In its golden flames,
something inside her released.
a tightness she hadn't realized she was holding.
Her shoulders softened.
Her calm deepened.
The dread drained from her body and into the earth.
Then, barely louder than the crackle of kindling,

She whispered–
"Thank you"

Finally,
    A release.
    A rush of relief so deep it filled her eyes.
    She would be warm.
    She would have light.
    Creatures of the dark would keep their distance.
    She would make it through.
    The trees watched
    and said nothing.
    But a breeze curled around her shoulder—
    an arm, gentle and unseen.
    And she remembered Jax's voice:
    "You're not missing anything down there.
    Look up.
    That's where you belong."
    So she looked up.
    And in the darkness between constellations,
    she thought she saw two lights sparkling side by side.
    Abuela and Jax.
    Still with her.
    She sat by the fire,
    knees tucked to her chest.
    The flames danced low and quiet,
    the way Jax had shown her—
    no smoke,
    just warmth.
    She fed it little twigs, one at a time.
    The fire flickered against the trees,
        pushing the dark back just enough to make her feel not quite so
small.

The fire didn't speak.

But it didn't leave, either.

And that was something.

She stared into the flames until her thoughts blurred at the edges.

Her thoughts slowed.

And in the quiet,

memories crept in—

not loud or sharp,

just faint flashes of before.

Abuela's arms.

Jax's shoulders.

The way the stars feel like friends.

Her heart ached with missing them.

"I'm doing it," the words barely escaped her lips.

She wasn't sure who she was talking to—

maybe the fire.

Maybe the star.

Maybe herself.

"But if You're listening..."

Her voice cracked,

barely a sound.

"Please... show me I'm going the right way.

Show me this path isn't a mistake.

I just need to know you see me.

That you haven't left."

She waited.

No thunder.

No voice from the clouds.

Just the sound of the wind threading through the trees.

Just the fire,

flickering low.

And still—

she waited.

Then a thought wove its way into her mind— gentle and sure–
as if carried by the wind or sent from the earth itself:

Maybe the bravest thing was asking for a sign at all...
    And still daring to believe it might come.

Myla lay beneath a canopy of stars.
She settled into the earth—
a seed before spring,
quiet,
unseen,
but full of what might come.
She curled closer to the warmth.
Not because she was cold—
but because it hurt a little less that way.
Sleep tugged at her—
a tide,
steady and slow.
But somewhere between the flicker of firelight and the hush of
her breath,
    sleep pulled her under.

Then, she opened her eyes...
    She was somewhere else.
    She was standing in a field of wild grass.
    But it wasn't the forest.
    The sky above her was the color of honeyed twilight,
    with stars that moved like slow fish through water.
    The wind carried the scent of pine,
    and everything blurred slightly at the edges,
    like a dream
    half-remembered.
    She turned—

and there he was.
Jax.
Not older.
Not younger.
Just him—exactly the way she remembered.
He was wearing the coat with the missing button.
His hands were in his pockets.
His smile was soft.
Myla ran to him.
He caught her in his arms—
the way only someone who sees you can.
He cupped her face in both hands,
gentle and steady.

"I'm proud of you" he said,

with his voice low with quiet intensity and certainty.
He wasn't just telling her.
he was offering her a truth to hold onto.
To know that he believed in her...
and maybe, just maybe that meant she could believe in herself too.

She wept—not because she was sad,
but because everything in her heart stopped aching all at once.
She was a flower growing in the shade—
quiet,
unseen,
still reaching.
touched by sunlight for the first time.
The words were life—giving light.
Not just heard,
felt.
And her tears weren't sorrow.

They were recognition.
A quiet *yes* from deep within her—
the part of her that had waited all her life
to know she was enough.
She felt a warmth she hadn't known she needed,
falling over every part of her that had waited too long.
The words didn't just comfort her.
They found her.
She heard the sacred words swirling in her aching spirit,
and they echoed through the deep places of her heart:
I'm proud of you.
I'm proud of you.
I'm proud of you.

Not a memory.
Not a thought.
But a truth she kept repeating to herself—
softly, steadily—
as if saying it enough times might finally make it real.
They healed her like medicine—
filling in the cracks,
And softening the ache.
She was looking down.
He reached out and placed a finger beneath her chin,
lifting her gaze.
She tilted her head up,
eyes full, heart open.
And when she met his eyes, she saw it.
He meant it.
Every word.
And in that moment, all she could say was—

"Thank you."

Because something inside her opened,
not in pain, but in recognition.
As if every part of her had been waiting
for this one moment of being seen...
and finally was.
"Are you real?" she said, barely daring to believe it.
"As real as you need me to be," he said, his half smile full of
mischief and moonlight.
She pulled back, looked up at him.
His eyes sparkled—
playful, and full of stars,
as always.
"I don't know if I can do this," She said.
Jax's smile didn't fade.
"You don't have to know.
 You just have to climb."
Then he tilted his head, studying her face.
And in the silence that followed,
 he asked the question she hadn't known she was waiting for:

"What would you do if you were me?"

She froze.
It was the kind of question that hung in the air,
heavy with meaning.
He was asking—not just what path she would choose,
but what kind of person she would be if she stood in his place.
If the world asked her to be the one who stayed strong.
To hold the truth.
To carry the light even when it cost everything.
She wanted to answer.
But she didn't know how.
"I... I don't know," she said.
His smile softened, and his eyes—

so full of love it steadied something inside her—
held hers without wavering.
Then, gently, he touched her cheek.
"You will," he said.
And somehow, she could feel it—
not just the words,
but the quiet assuredness
behind them.
As if he had already seen who she was becoming,
and believed in her completely.

She didn't yet understand—
but something inside her had begun to awaken—
Quiet and deep,
dawn touching the edges of a sleeping world
nd Jax faded.
His presence dissolving into the moonlight.
But the question he asked lingered,
a quiet thread winding through her soul,
would follow her up the mountain.

Myla woke with tears in her eyes and frost on her lashes.
The stars were still overhead.
Her star barely glimmered–
as if it, too,
was struggling to find hope in the silence.
Her heart ached in response,
knowing it was waiting for her,
but unsure if she could reach it.
She spoke softly into the stillness,
"I think I understand."
And she stood.

The first light of dawn began to creep over the horizon,
painting the sky in soft shades of pink, orange and gold.
Myla watched the sunrise as she walked,
her steps steady and sure,
each one bringing her closer to the truth she had been seeking.
The quiet beauty of the morning echoed the change within her.
The world was waking.
And so was she.

hapter Three: The Voice Like Velvet

The path narrowed between two ancient stone spires,
  dark with moss and mist.
  The air grew heavier,
  As if it carried too many thoughts.
  Myla's breath came slower now.
  The forest no longer felt wild–
  but watchful.
  She had walked for hours without seeing another living thing.
  Until the feathers came.
  One by one,

black feathers drifted from the branches above—
silent, perfect, shining like ink.
Myla's breath caught.

A raven.
    The first living thing she'd seen since the village.
    It landed on a low branch just ahead,
    its feathers glowing faintly brushed with starlight in motion.

"Hello," she said,
        voice catching on hope,
        wrapped in wonder.
    She stepped closer,
    her heart racing.
    "You're... beautiful."
    The raven blinked once,
        slow and deliberate—
    and the sky seemed to flicker with him.
    He angled his head sideways and studied her face,
    Then, a voice—not out loud, but inside her thoughts, curling soft
as smoke:
    You've come far, little one.
    Her chest swelled.
    Someone had noticed. Someone was here.
    "Who are you?" she asked, eyes wide.
    An old friend, the raven answered.
    Sent by one who loved you.
    My name is Jeval.
    He told me to protect you, you know,
    he said, eyes gleaming.
    Jax, He said you were precious.

· · ·

Myla's breath caught.
Her heart ached.
"Jax?"
The name fell from her lips, a memory–
Fragile,
aching,
real.
A sign.
A real sign.
Her eyes welled.
Her hands trembled.

And then—
The raven stepped down from the branch,
talons clicking softly against the bark.
And as he moved,
he began to change—
not vanishing,
but unfolding.
The raven's image rippled—
then blurred,
As if the night itself were bending.
Slowly it began to stretch.
Feathers folded into fingers.
Wings curled into arms.
A man took shape from myth and shadow—
cloaked in black,
feathers braided into hair gleaming with starlight.
She felt an uneasy feeling in her stomach.
His voice was kind,
it stirred something half—buried in her—
part memory,
part longing.

She didn't quite have words for it.
Not yet.

"You knew him?" Myla said, the ache curling just beneath her heart.
Jeval nodded solemnly.

Then Jeval spoke.
Not in thought.
Not in whispers.
But aloud–
To the forest,
To the trees
and to her.
Everyone heard.
She heard.
His voice was like velvet.
"He spoke of you often.
Said you were fire and stardust.
Said he couldn't protect you anymore... but I could."

Myla's knees weakened.
This was the first time anyone-anything-had spoken Jax's name since she left.
"I miss him," she murmured faintly.

Jeval stepped closer.
"Then let me carry you the rest of the way.
You're tired.
The mountain is steep.
And truth?"

His smile curled.
"No one's waiting at the top."

She wanted to believe him.
    His voice was warm.
    His presence, familiar.
    He knew things about her–
    things no one else could possibly know.
    They stood in silence.
    Jeval smiled,
    soft and measured.
    But something about it made her pause.
    He was a little too pleased.
    She didn't know why,
    but the back of her neck prickled—
    As though something unseen had crept closer.

And then it began.
    His eyes locked onto hers—
    Obsidian,
    endless,
    glinting with something ancient.
    Not flame.
    Not shadow.
    Something in between.
    They weren't just watching her.
    They were pulling her in.
    A spiral of stillness.
    A mirror of doubt.
    Her thoughts slowed.
    Her breath shallowed.
    It was as if his gaze was not just looking through her—

but unraveling her.
Her legs slowed.
Her eyelids tugged downward—
not from sleep,
but from something heavier than thought.
Everything around her dissolved—
She sank,
water rising in her ears,
sealing her in silence.
Her head felt heavy,
too heavy to lift.
Her thoughts drifted in and out,
none of them fully forming,
as though her
thoughts were underwater,
rising for breath but never quite breaking the surface.
His words curled around her,
smoke—
delicate,
vanishing,
and impossible to hold.
She wanted to believe him—
wanted it so badly
the wanting itself brought her to a precipice,
where belief became surrender,
Her eyes dimmed,
her heart drifting,
and the next step wasn't trust,
but oblivion.
She was floating inside herself,
numb with grief,
and Jeval could feel it
He could feel the weight settling in her bones.
He leaned in–

not with kindness
but with timing.
She took one step toward him toward the edge.
"You've done enough," he murmured,
"Let it go. You can rest now."
The words slithered around her,
a serpent made of smoke—
dark,
slow and sure.
they coiled,
over her skin,
and slipped into her breath
with an invitation to surrender.
And she almost did...
She almost surrendered to the velvet lie.
But somewhere inside her,
a sacred truth emerged—
words she didn't recognize as her own:

This one speaks poison in poetry.
    Don't drink from his voice.

A shriek tore through the trees.
Sharp.
Clear.
Cutting through the illusion
like a blade.
A blur of white and silver from the sky—
feathers streaked with lightning.
The white owl struck Jeval mid-step,
sending a storm of feathers into the air.
He staggered,
snarled,
and hissed—

but she circled back around
and landed between him and Myla,
wings wide, eyes blazing.

"Enough!," the owl said.

Jeval's form splintered, flickered—
and collapsed into a whirlwind of dark feathers
that scattered on the wind.
Silence returned.
Myla fell to her knees.
She didn't know whether to cry, scream or thank the stars.

The owl walked to her, slow and regal.
She didn't offer a wing to lean on.
She perched on a branch just above,
wings folding in with quiet grace.
Her presence didn't just arrive—it radiated.
Warmth poured from her, sunlight through trees,
Surrounding Myla in a hush of radiant peace.
Before she spoke,
Myla felt herself exhale—
A breath held for what seemed an eternity.
"I'm Themis, she said.
 The star sent me to protect you."
"That voice, Themis said softly, feeds on love you haven't
healed."
Myla looked down.
"It felt like him. Like Jax."
Themis nodded.
"That's how it works.

It doesn't lie outright.
It twists what's sacred until it breaks you."

They sat in silence for a long while.
 Then Themis turned to her.
 "You have the bones of a warrior."
 But bones break unless they are strengthened."
 Myla stood before Themis,
 her heart pounding with both fear and excitement.
 The owl watched her with eyes full of ancient wisdom,
 its presence both steady and ethereal,
 emanating a quiet,
 powerful energy.
 "You are not alone, Myla," the owl said,
 its voice soft but firm,
 carrying the weight of centuries.
 "But you must trust in yourself.
 There is a power in you,
 one that will guide you when the path grows unclear."
 "Take this."
 The owl extended her wing,
 and nestled within the feathers was a small, delicate crystal—
 clear but strange,
 with a deep shimmer,
 like the reflection of an owl's eye.
 The light within it seemed to shift,
 as though it held a hidden truth that Myla had yet to understand.
 Myla took the crystal into her trembling hands,
 feeling a warmth radiate from it.
 It wasn't heavy,
 but it felt important
 as though it was alive with potential.
 There was something waiting within it.

"This will guide you," the owl said,
its eyes filled with ancient knowing.
"When you are lost, when you feel unsteady, hold this.
 It will help you find your way."
Uncertain of the full meaning, but feeling the crystal's power
resonate within her.
She tucked it away,
feeling its warmth emanating from her satchel.
Themis and the crystal were a part of her now, companions on
her journey.
"When the time is right, I will return," Themis said.

That night, she didn't dream.
The forest held her in stillness.
And the star above?
It pulsed—
Not brightly,
Not boldly...
What reached her wasn't a dream.
It was deeper.
Not a voice.
Not a vision.
But an awakened truth behind her mind's eye.
Myla stepped closer,
and in the hush between heartbeats,
she heard it.
Not with her ears.
Not with her mind.
But in the place where knowing lives.
And the star spoke—not in words, but in memory, in light:

    I did not forget you.
    I dimmed to survive.

I buried my voice in silence so it would not be stolen.
But I have felt your footsteps.
And I know you're close.

And as Myla heard the star's voice—
soft and unguarded—
Something began to unwind inside her.
They found each other in the silence—
not as savior and saved,
but as reflections of the same wound.
The star had dimmed to protect its light.
Myla had done the same
and now, together, they began to remember...
not just who they were—But the light they were always meant to
become.

C hapter Four: The Bargain of Shadows

Daylight broke through the mist,
    soft and tentative.
    Myla awoke slowly,
    her body heavy with tiredness,
    the morning light gently pulling her from slumber.
    The weight of the night's silence lifted,
    replaced by the quiet murmur of the forest around her.
    The air,
    now fresher,
    seemed to pulse with new life,
    but Myla carried the heaviness of the path ahead.
    The stone spires rose like a silent sentinel,
    casting shadows that hinted of what she might yet face.
    The sun rose slowly,
    painting the forest path in amber.
    She sat up,

reaching into her satchel for the small bundle of bread
and dried berries she had wrapped tightly in cloth.
Her stomach growled in quiet protest–
she hadn't eaten much the day before,
and the bread was stale,
but it was sustenance.
The berries were tart,
a small reminder of the forest's gifts,
but she chewed slowly,
trying to savor what little she had.
Myla didn't mind the hunger–
it was a part of the journey.
But the fatigue was starting to creep in,
and she knew she couldn't push herself much longer without
replenishing what energy she had left.
She hungered for more,
 but she put the small remnants of the bread back into her
satchel for later
and her fingers brushed against the smooth,
warm surface of the owl's—eye crystal.
She didn't need to look at it.
She felt it—the crystal seemed to hum with a life of its own,
its presence was more than just an object.
It was a bridge,
a link between her and the wisdom of Themis,
a power that resonated gently under her fingers.
And the spiral galaxy locket rested heavy on her chest.
The image of the swirling stars was etched into its surface,
and it seemed to shift in the light.
Sometimes,
when the ache inside grew too loud,
she would take her index finger
and trace the spiral galaxy etched into the charm—
slowly, softly—

until the world was quiet again.
As she traced the spiral galaxy with her finger,
she realized—
she wasn't alone.
The world was alive with magic,
with forces beyond her understanding,
and she was a part of it all.
Myla walked in silence,
the token from Themis in her satchel for safe keeping.
She was tired—more than tired.
Her muscles ached,
her feet blistered,
and her stomach curled in on itself from hunger.
The dream of Jax,
the battle with Jeval,
the weight of the mountain–
it all pressed down on her.
And that's when the path began to change.
The forest thinned.
The air warmed.
And golden leaves began to fall–
not from trees,
but from the sky itself,
drifting as if time had slowed.
Ahead, a fire crackled.
A kettle steamed.
A woven blanket lay on soft grass,
beside a wood table set with honeyed bread,
steaming tea,
and fruit she hadn't tasted since childhood.
Myla blinked.
He appeared.

. . .

A fox,

    tall and graceful,

    fur the color of sunset and silver thread.

    His eyes reflected like mirrors,

    always reflecting her back to herself.

    He bowed low,

    one paw sweeping the ground.

    "Hello"he said... with a grin so warm it could melt snow,

    "You've arrived.

    Finally."

    She didn't move.

    "Who are you?"

    "A friend."

    My name is Dastan.

    He gestured to the blanket.

    "Sit. Eat. You've come so far.

    Let someone take care of you now."

    Her hunger clawed at her.

    Her knees trembled.

    But she didn't sit.

    Not yet.

"What do you want?" she asked.

    Dastan laughed.

    "Nothing.

    Truly.

    You're a guest, not a captive.

    But... if you're asking what I offer..."

    He stepped closer, lowering his voice as if he was telling her a secret:

    "Rest.

    An ending.

    Peace.

You don't have to finish the climb.
You've already proven your courage.
Just take what you've earned.
I'll draw you a map back down—safe, easy, quiet.
You can start again somewhere new.
Isn't that what you really want?
You've already been through so much.
Why make it harder than it has to be?"

Myla's body ached with want.
The tea smelled of clove and safety.
The bread reminded her of her Abuela's oven.
The offer made sense.
It wasn't cruel.
It was kind.
Reasonable.
She took one step toward the blanket.
Then stopped.
Because something about Dastan's smile didn't reach his eyes.
Myla hesitated.

She slowly took the crystal out of the satchel and held it in her pocket.
Her stomach growled and her heart was unsettled.
The token—the owl's eye crystal–
pressed against her palm,
warm and alive.
Her fingers clenched the token in her pocket,
a reminder of everything she had been taught by Themis.
As her hand wrapped around the crystal, its warmth flowed into her.

. . .

For a moment,
    everything slowed.
    The tempting bread before her blurred,
    and in the haze of that moment,
    her vision cleared.
    She looked at the loaf more closely,
    and suddenly,
    the bread wasn't fresh anymore.
    It was covered in mold—
    decaying, spoiled.
    The comfort Dastan offered was no longer warm;
    it was a rotting illusion,
    a false hope that could never truly satisfy her.
    Themis' voice echoed in her mind, steady and clear:
    Do not be deceived by what seems easy.
    True nourishment comes with growth, not avoidance.
    Myla stood up straighter,
    shaking off the fog of temptation.
    She looked at Dastan,
    the warmth of the crystal still in her hand,
    and the strength of her own truth began to rise within her.
    Something stirred in her— an echo buried deep,
    It rose:
    the memory of a dream,
    quiet but clear.

He'd asked her once,
    in that dream—
    What would you do if you were me?
    It wasn't about his question anymore.
    It was about her answer.
    Now she had it.
    She bit the words out through clenched teeth,

too low for even Dastan to hear.
But they weren't his to hear.

"I'd keep going."

Because it was love—
love for Jax,
Love for the dream where he came to her,
And the memory that never left.
Love that has waited in her heart,
Patiently.
Because it knew it would come back someday.
Love reached the places even courage had left untouched.
She didn't speak it.
She didn't have to.
She looked up at Dastan,
calm but resolute—
her energy steady and unmistakable.
It filled the space between them before she even spoke.
She didn't rush.
She let the stillness speak first.

"No," Myla said, steady and sure.
    "I won't be fooled by comfort that hides decay.
I don't need your bread.
I don't need shortcuts.
And now I know— I don't just believe.
I've found my own strength."

Dastan's smile faltered,
    his eyes hardening,
    but Myla didn't flinch.

She knew now that true strength didn't come from avoiding struggle–
    it came from facing it with clarity.
    The tea had gone cold.
    And beneath the gold leaf littering the path—there were bones.
    Half—buried in moss and time.
    Her breath stopped.
    Not from fear—
    from recognition.
    Something inside her—
    deep and wordless—
    Froze.

This is what happened
    to the ones who said yes.
    Myla stared at him.
    "Why are you in such a rush to end my story?"
    Dastan didn't answer.
    His smile remained frozen.
    "You don't want me to rest," she said.
    "You want me to give up."
    She stepped back.
    "I'd rather walk with nothing than settle for a lie."
    The fox blinked once—twice—and vanished in a whisper of smoke and gold.

Myla fell to her knees and wept.
    Not because she was broken.
    But because she had chosen not to be.
    The forest held her in stillness.

C hapter Five: The Flame of Clarity

Myla stayed there for a long time,
    curled beside the path where Dastan's illusions had vanished,
    knees pressed to earth.
    The air around her was still heavy with his words.
    Then—slowly—she rose.

The forest had darkened again.
    branches stretched overhead—
    fingers reaching through shadow.

Now, even the birds were quiet.
She walked until the air grew thin and sharp.
The path turned rocky,
hugging the edge of a cliff.
And just when she thought she could go no further,
she saw it:

A hollow in the stone.
Half hidden by tangled vines and glowing moss,
a cave opened—
a breath in the mountain's chest.
She stepped inside.
It wasn't cold.
It was warm.
Dry.
Lit from within by the faint flicker of ancient firelight that had no
source.
The walls were etched with symbols–
spirals,
wings,
stars,
and rising flames.
The air smelled of smoke
and something older than memory.
It wasn't a shelter.
It was a sanctuary.
Myla knelt in the center of the cave,
feeling the mountain's heartbeat beneath her palms.

And that's when she heard it.
The wind changed.
And with it,

came a shimmer of silver light.
Themis.
She stepped forward from the edge of the cave,
her feathers sleek,
her eyes sharp as glass.
She didn't speak at first.
She only looked at Myla–
closely,
deeply–
then nodded.
"You saw through him," she said. "That's no small thing."
Myla lowered her gaze.
"But I almost didn't."
Themis tilted her head.
"That's how it works."
The closer you are to truth, the more beautiful the lies become."

She circled Myla once.
"Your heart is strong," she said,
"but your mind is still clouded.
Fear fogs your clarity.
Let's change that."
She lowered her head to Myla's brow.
And when their foreheads touched–
Visions swirled through Myla's mind.
She saw the moments she had doubted herself.
The times her voice was silenced.
When shame clung to her—a second skin.
When they told her she was imagining it all.
When her truth was twisted until even she questioned it.
When she was made to feel small,
unseen,
and unworthy.

When they tried to erase what she knew deep in every fiber of
her being.
   And one by one,
   those thoughts shattered like glass.

When she opened her eyes,
   It was as if her mind had been sharpened to a blade's edge.
   Myla didn't speak.
   She couldn't.
   The cave held its breath.
   And so did she.

Then—
   the heat came.
   Not sudden.
   Not sharp.
   A slow rise,
   The air had thickened with memory.
   It curled around her ankles,
   climbed her spine,
   and settled behind her ribs.
   She turned—
   not because she heard anything,
   but because she felt it.
   The air was glowing.
   The flame on the far wall of the cave morphed—
   not flickering.
   but becoming.
   It stretched.
   Lengthened.
   Pooled into shape.
   Light expanded across stone

And slowly–
As though the fire was remembering itself–
The Phoenix began to take form.
Wings unfolded—
massive,
radiant,
endless.
Feathers emerged from flame,
each one alive with color and heat.
It didn't walk.
It moved as fire itself—
fluid,
alive,
hypnotic.
Its feathers iridesced with every color Myla had ever seen and
some she hadn't.
Golds, crimsons, deep cosmic blues.
A mythic fire—
a dance of truth
and resurrection.

Myla couldn't move.
She didn't want to.
She stood inside a dream,
watching the most beautiful sunrise she had ever seen—
not on the horizon,
but from within it.
Face—to—face
with something ancient
And luminous—
a force that remembered the beginning of all things.
A being made of heat, energy, memory and mercy.
it danced—

Not with fury,
but with reverence.
A sacred,
spiraling rhythm.
The flames rose
and circled her—
not to burn,
but to reveal.
And in their center,
Myla saw the lie.

She saw herself as a child.
Not on the mountain.
Not in the forest.
But in a room.
With him.
Her real father.
Not Jax—the soul who gave without asking—
but the man whose voice had carved doubt into her bones.
He said the soul searing words:

You'll never have anything to offer the world.

The words didn't just hurt.
They branded her—soul deep, bone close.
And she had believed him.
Not because it was true—
but because she needed his love to mean something.
Even if it hurt.

The Phoenix circled faster now—
not punishing,

but purifying.
Its fire curled around the memory,
lifting it,
The flames wrapped around the memory—
not to destroy it,
but to alchemize it.
It didn't vanish.
It changed.
She saw the words again—

You'll never have anything to offer the world.

But they weren't sharp anymore.
They weren't cutting.
They were glowing.
The fire held them—
heated them,
purified them,
turned them from iron into gold.
This was not erasure.
This was reclamation.
The lie had not been burned away.
It had been rewritten
in flame.
It became the depth of her empathy,
the root of her courage,
The words were rewritten:

I have something to offer the world—
because I survived the part of it that told me I wouldn't.

All that doubt,
all that silence,
all that struggle—

became her offering.
The fire didn't steal her past.
It honored it.
It forged it into truth.

Without warning,
    Myla stepped forward.
    She danced.
    With the Phoenix.
    With the fire.
    With everything she had once feared.
    The flames wrapped around her—
    and when they receded,
    the memory was gone.
    Not forgotten.
    Transformed.
    She was still Myla—
    but something in her ignited.
    She was no longer carrying the lie.
    She was no longer asking for permission to shine.

The Phoenix bowed.
A single feather loosened from its wing—
drifting slowly to the ground.
Myla picked it up.
It was warm.
Not burning,
but alive—
And she put it in her satchel.
Something in her had begun to stir—
not fully awakened,
but no longer asleep.
There was a warmth within her now—
not from forgetting the pain,
but from moving through it.
Embers waiting
for the breath that would turn them to flame.

The cave fell still.
And Myla stood at the center,
newborn in her own skin.
Themis bowed to her head slightly.
"You've been given what few are ever offered:

Clarity of mind,
    and fire of spirit."

Myla didn't know what would come next.
But she was no longer afraid.
She sat down by the fire,
watching it dance in slow,
hypnotic waves.
The flames flickered,
a drumbeat,

casting weaving light and shadow across the stones.
She didn't try to name the thoughts.
They came as quiet tides—
memories,
questions,
fragments of something older than words.
The fire held them all without judgment.
At some point,
her eyes grew heavy,
The warmth of the moment still wrapped around her.
And before she could make sense of it all,
Sleep gathered her gently in its arms.
That night,
she slept curled against the temple's wall,
the spiral galaxy locket pressed close to her heart.
And she dreamed.
She was standing in a glowing meadow that belonged to no place on earth,
Yet it held a deeper sense of home than anywhere she had ever known.
The stars hung low–
Close enough to pluck—
ancient fruit from the cosmos.
And there,
beneath a sky alive with luminescence,
stood her Abuela.
Smiling.
Arms open.

"Mija" her voice wrapped in love.
Myla ran to her.
Her Abuela's arms were warm.
Clove and Jasmine. It was her.

It was home.

"You've grown so strong," she said.

"So bright."

"I miss you," Myla said into her chest.

"I know," Abuela said, touching the locket around Myla's neck.

"But I never left.

This..."—she traced the spiral–

"is not just a galaxy. It's a map. A reminder."

"A reminder of what?"

Her Abuela smiled.

"That you carry the whole universe inside you."

Myla closed her eyes.

When she woke,

the Phoenix was gone.

But the fire remained.

C hapter Six: The Pathkeeper of Fear

Dawn came in silence.

Not the kind that brings peace.

The kind that waits.

Myla left the fire-temple with the Phoenix's feather tucked into her satchel

and her Abuela's locket close to her chest.

The air had changed.

Crisper.

Thinner.

The mountain no longer curved–

it climbed,

steep

and sharp,

The path narrowed to a ledge carved straight into stone.

And that's where she saw him.

· · ·

Wolf.

He stood directly in her way,

tall and gray,

fur dusted with frost,

eyes cold and unblinking.

He didn't growl.

He didn't bare his teeth.

He simply stood.

Between her

and the next step.

Myla stopped.

The silence between them stretched so long,

it began to feel alive.

Without moving his mouth,

Wolf spoke.

Not aloud.

But inside her.

You cannot pass.

Her pulse slowed.

Not from calm—but from warning.

It's too risky, he said. *You'll break.*

She stepped forward.

He moved one pace to the side—

still blocking the path.

Myla took a breath.

Her voice cracked.

"Why are you doing this?"

Wolf's eyes never changed.

Her heart stung like a struck bell.

*There's no place for you, child, up there...*he said flatly.

No plan.

No protection.

Walk away now, or you will suffer the aftermath.

"You're lying."
   No, Wolf said, with quiet precision. *I'm withholding.*
   He didn't need to deceive.
   He didn't shout.
   He didn't twist her memories or tempt her with softness.
   He simply blocked her path–
   with silence,
   with red-tinted fear,
   with a wall of calm that said:
   You don't get to move forward.
   Because I said so.

Myla's hands curled into fists.
   This was different than Jeval's velvet voice,
   or Dastan's honeyed lies.
   This was power without warmth.
   This was logic without love.
   This was the world telling her,
   without apology:
   You don't belong here.
   And for a moment—
   She believed it.
   For just one moment, her knees began to give.
   But then—
   She heard Themis's voice:

   Fear fogs your clarity.

And Jax's words, rising from memory—
  fire from ash:

I'll always be there for you. You know that.

  Myla stood taller.
  She looked Wolf in the eyes.
  And when she spoke, her voice wasn't just hers.
  It was the voice of every ancestor that had ever risen against darkness.
  It wasn't loud.
  But it was unbreakable.

"You don't get to tell me who I become."

  The mountain heard her.
  And it trembled.
  Not with anger.
  But with recognition.
  The stones beneath her stirred—
  The mountain rose in defiance, shielding her.
  The wind roared up the cliffs.
  And Wolf—frozen, silent, unshakable—moved.
  Not because she forced him.
  But because the mountain had chosen her.

Myla passed him.
  Not in defiance.
  In power.
  She paused at the edge of the path,
  the weight of Wolf's words still pressing against her chest.
  But she didn't fall.
  She didn't crumble or weep.

Instead, she closed her eyes.
She straightened her back,
opened her fists,
and tilted her head to the sky.
Sunlight warmed her cheeks.
She drew the breath in slowly—
through her nose,
and released it through her mouth like a vow.
And for the first time,
she didn't feel the weight of the world pressing down on her—
she sensed it moving through her.
It was no longer a burden.
It was her power.
The power of her own choice,
of refusing to be silenced.
And once she was beyond him,
she did not look back.

C hapter Seven: The Cry of the Star

The air was thin.
  Too thin.
  Myla climbed in silence,
  her boots scraping against stone.
  The trees had vanished.
  The sky was too close.
  The summit was near—
  just beyond the last ridge.

. . .

And that's when she appeared.

A figure walking calmly down the path.

Not hurried.

Not weary.

Floating, almost.

She was beautiful—

achingly,

impossibly beautiful.

Her hair was dark black,

her dress woven from something that shimmered but did not shine.

Her face was a painting.

She looked at Myla with eyes that sparkled,

and for a moment,

Myla forgot where she was.

Forgot everything.

"You've made it far," the woman said,

her voice soft as silk.

"I've been watching."

She stepped closer, slowly—

an old friend returning from a long absence.

"Who are you?" Myla said.

"Someone who understands," she said.

"Someone who knows how much it hurts to keep climbing."

"I know what it is to carry too much," the woman sighed.

"To love so deeply it breaks you."

Myla blinked.

"You... do?"

The woman's gaze softened.

"Of course.

I've felt it too.

I tried to protect the ones I loved...

but no one ever saw that."

She took Myla's hands in hers—cool, graceful, elegant.
    Her touch was gentle, but her grip lingered too long—
    a vine that pretends to hold, but tightens.
    "You remind me of someone I used to be.
    Before the world hardened me.
    Before I had to become..."
    She trailed off.
    Myla's chest tightened.
    She felt it—the longing to believe her.
    The need to be seen, understood, forgiven.
    The woman pulled her close.
    "You don't have to keep fighting.
    You're safe now.
    I'll take care of you."
    She brushed the hair from Myla's face with a gentleness
    that should have felt comforting.
    And for a moment—it did.
    It felt exactly Myla had always longed for,
    something that brushed against the edge of motherly love.
    The kind that wrapped you in arms that asked for nothing.
    The kind that *whispered, rest now, you're safe.*
    And Myla—just for a heartbeat
    —wanted to believe it.
    More than anything.
    The ache was too old.
    Too deep.
    A child's wish buried in a warrior's chest.
    And before she could stop it—
    It rose up in her throat.

    "Just don't leave me."

It wasn't a plea.
It was a truth.
A fracture at the root.
She would've given it all away.
Her voice, her fire, her climb—
Just to be held.

And that is when the illusion cracked.
The woman's eyes sparkled too much—
glass catching firelight.
Then Myla saw it.
Not tenderness.
Not truth.
Hunger.
The kind that doesn't feed on food,
but on light.
Not for closeness.
For control.
She didn't want to comfort her.
She saw it in her eyes all at once:
She wanted to take what Myla held most precious–
her heart,
her fire,
her light–
and turn it into a weakness.
To exploit the love Myla gave freely,
twisting it into something fragile,
something that could be used against her.
She sought to make Myla feel that love was a burden–
wearing her down until she doubted the very strength that made
her shine.
She wanted to own her.
To undermine her fire.

And Myla's body went cold.

Because this was not sisterhood.

This was a kindness laced with poison,
 a trap dressed as love.

This was someone who would smile while cutting her from behind.

Then—

The ground tilted beneath her feet.

The moss beneath her pulsed and she was sinking.

And suddenly—

Myla was falling.

Not down a path.

Not through space.

But into herself.

Into a chasm carved by every time she had betrayed her own truth.

The world around her blurred,
 as if everything—every shape,
 every sound—was slipping through a veil of smoke,
 fading into nothingness.

She wasn't sure if her body was still there
 or if she had already fallen too far to feel it.

The weight of her own doubts pulled her deeper,
 each stone heavier than the last,
 dragging her down.

The enchantress' voice faded into the distance,
 a faint echo of words she couldn't quite grasp.

And Myla screamed.

But something else,
 something ancient,
 drifted back.

A flicker of light.

A breath of air.
A pulse of power.
A cry rose through the dark.
A cry of fire.
Wings.
The Phoenix burst from the void,
    trailing sparks and a blaze of gold, crimson, and red streaking
across the sky,
    catching Myla before the fall became final.
It didn't speak.
It didn't need to.
Its fire cradled her,
    lifting her,
    healing the cracks inside her that the hollow queen had tried to
break open.
    And when it placed her gently back on the path—
The woman was gone.
Returned to the summit dissolving into dusk.
Mask perfectly back in place.
But Myla had seen beneath it.
She stood.
Not broken.
Burning.

That's when she heard it.
    A sound not meant for ears,
     but for the soul.
    A sob from the sky.
    A sound that was not a sound.
    A voice that was not a voice.

The Star.

It was just ahead, visible now through the thinning air,
In the night sky—
a dying ember suspended between worlds.
It should have been radiant.
But it was dim.
Its glow ached—soft and strained,
as if it had waited in silence for so long,
it had almost forgotten why... until now.
And somehow,
without a single word,
they understood each other.
The star's sorrow mirrored her own.
And Myla,
without knowing how,
knew it had been waiting for her all along.
And from it—
Tears of stardust fell,
trailing down in silver flame,
landing on the mountain's peak and searing the stone.
The star was crying.
And as it wept,
the mountain burned and crackled,
the ground beneath her feet searing with every step.
Each tear struck the mountain,
burning the earth—
a quiet wail,
a low moan of sorrow that seeped into stone.
Myla ran,
every step a battle against the heat rising from the mountain—
thick, heavy, and unrelenting.
The ground beneath her feet pulsed.
She dodged each tear as it struck the earth,
each one hissing on contact—
grief-made molten—

before the next one fell.
Myla gasped,
the grief came in waves—
a storm that was clawing at her chest,
making her legs shake beneath her.
"Yes", she said and her voice shook.
"I hear you.
I know what it is to be forgotten."

The star throbbed low, with a quiet ache.
   "Help..."
It was a plea, soft but desperate.
The mountain mourned.
And so did the star.
And Myla understood.
She wasn't just here to rise.
She was here to free the star.
To fulfill its wishes.
To keep it from vanishing.
And somewhere deep in her,
she began to realize—
She was one with it.

Chapter Eight: The Sisters Who Fracture The Light

At last, Myla reached the peak.
    There, chained in silence, hovered the star.
    It barely flickered now.
    Its glow dimmed by sorrow
    and she saw them.
    Two women stood beside the star–

The Captors.

And then it hit her—

The moment you begin to rise, resistance will come. Not because you are wrong, but because the parts of the world that fear light will try to extinguish it.

She hadn't just been climbing a mountain—
she had been climbing through every voice that ever tried to pull her back down.
Through doubt.
Through silence.
Through the fear of being too much.
But she was done shrinking.
She wasn't here to be understood.
She was here to remember who she was.

Myla gasped.
They looked like reflections of each other...
twisted in different directions.
 Like a single coin seen from both sides
—opposite in shape, but forged from the same wound.

Aurelia—radiant and poised,
every movement choreographed,
every word a performance.
Her beauty was breathtaking–
until you looked too long.
Then it shattered into artifice.
Her beauty was a costume,
built on lies she told the world.

The other—Eris
—was unraveling.

Her hair hung in strands,
her eyes were heavy with lost time.
She didn't try to lie to the world
She had lied to herself for so long,
she no longer remembred what was real.
Her pain had hardened into cruelty.

Myla staggered back,
her chest still tight from the spell Aurelia had poured into her.
It had wrapped around her mind, a web—
seductive and suffocating,
folding her in on herself until she nearly disappeared.
If the Phoenix hadn't come when he did...
She didn't want to think about what would've happened.
Her hands were still shaking.
Her knees felt hollow.
But something deeper—older—rose inside her.
She met Aurelia's gaze.

"Why do you care if the star shines?" Myla asked.
Aurelia's smile cracked.
Eris flinched.
"Because when people wish," Aurelia hissed, "They hope and when they hope, they believe they can rise. We rose once and we shattered."
She stepped closer,
her voice glinting with menace—
sharp and sweet, like honey laced with glass.
"I was everything the world said I should be," Aurelia said.
"Beautiful.
Worshipped.
They did everything for me.

Gave me what I wanted before I even had to ask.
"I made people want me,"Aurelia said.
"They gave me things."
Followed me.
"I was the center of every room.
Isn't that love?"
Her voice caught for half a second, but she smoothed it away.
"They adored me. They listened."
What else is there?"
Her eyes turned toward the star, then narrowed.
"But you know what happens to people who try to rise too high?
They fall and when they fall, No one catches them.
That's what hope does.
 It tricks you into thinking someone will."

Eris' voice came low,
 from the shadows.
"I don't even remember what I asked the star for
or maybe I do and I just don't want to admit it."
She tilted her head, eyes glassy.
"Maybe I wanted to feel whole.
Maybe I thought the starlight would erase the parts of me I
hated."
She smiled, and it was more terrifying than anger.
"It didn't."

Aurelia stepped beside her,
 their figures darkened and twisted—
two opposing forces–
each one pulling,
each one pushing.
"We gave everything once," Aurelia said.

"We believed in something brighter.
And it broke us."
She glanced at Eris,
whose silence trembled with memory.
"So now—we guard the mountain.
We stop the dreamers."
We unmake the story before it dares to bloom."
Her voice dropped—sharp and sorrowed, almost tender.
"It's mercy, really. Hope is a trick—
a lie dressed in starlight."
We're only keeping others from climbing to the same height...
just to fall."

Maya felt the chill of those words—
how close they came to sounding kind.
But that was the danger.
That was the trap.
Right before you rise into your full self,
you will be tested by forces that sound wise—
but are really the voice of your oldest fear,
asking you to stay small.
They're not enemies.
They're thresholds.
And if you don't name them for what they are,
they will win.
They were the final guardians of her own doubt,
cloaked in the illusion of reason,
the last gate before initiation into her full self.
And she would not bow to them.

Myla stood in silence.
Not out of fear—

but because there was nothing left to say.

The truth sat there, ugly and obvious–and still they did not
see it.

She finally understood.

They weren't monsters.

They were what becomes of love–

left to grow in the shadow

of its own unmet longing.

When wounds grow teeth.

When the mask becomes the only face you remember.

They had built their cage out of choices,

one heartbreak at a time.

And now they lived in it so long,

they couldn't tell the difference

between protection and control.

Between helping and harming.

Between love... and power.

She felt it rise in her—

a tide swelling from within.

Not rage.

Not pity.

Just revelation.

They were broken.

And she might have been too,

if not for Jax,

if not for her abuela,

if not for love that had held her when she was lost.

But now—

their brokenness was no longer just theirs.

It was hurting the star.

It was hurting every wish still hanging in the sky.

She saw them.

She mourned them.
But she did not owe them understanding.
She had come to set the star free.
And nothing—
not their sorrow,
not their story—
would stop her.
They were guarding their own brokenness.
and calling it truth.

Aurelia—sharp,
   gilded,
Hollow.
A woman who turned her need into a throne.
A queen of mirrors.
The empress in a palace of praise–
draped in illusion,
blind to her own nakedness.
Eris—weathered,
bitter,
lost.
A woman who forgot the sound of her own voice.
Not because it was taken—
Because she gave it away,
   piece by piece,
   to survive.

Together, they had become the gate.
   Not because they were chosen.
   But because no one else was willing to stay with them.
   Not because the world turned away,
   but because they had built walls around themselves.

They had been left behind.
Their pain had become a throne,
and no one would sit beside them.
They didn't hate the light —
they feared it.
Because it reminded them of what they had lost.
What they had chosen to lose.
They feared it.
Because it showed them what they had become.
So they chose to extinguish it—
One dreamer at a time.

Myla stepped forward.
The mountain trembled beneath her feet.
Not in protest.
In support.
She touched the spiral locket around her neck.
The fire of the phoenix still flickered in her chest.
She spoke.

"You don't understand love," she said.
"You think it abandoned you, but love doesn't chain what it can't control.
You broke because you forgot who you are."

Aurelia flinched.
Eris' mouth tightened.
"You don't know what we've lost," Aurelia growled.
Myla stepped closer.
"You're right," She said.
"I don't know what you lost, but I know what I won't lose."
She turned to the star.
It murmured once—faint, but still alive.

and in that moment, she felt it:
Not just this star—but all of them.
A deep ache stretching across the sky.
A silent weeping in every constellation.
When one star is chained, they all suffer.
Because they are not separate.
They are a family of light.
A breath of the same soul.
and she—she was one with them.
Myla reached up.
The chains hissed as her hand drew near.
The sisters stepped forward in unison.
"Don't!" they said.
Myla stood before the chain, her heart a heavy drumbeat in her
chest.

Every part of her wanted to turn away,
to leave it all behind—
except she knew she couldn't.
Not anymore.
She had seen the truth.
She saw through the lies—
the weight of the world's injustices pressing in on her
and this time,
she wouldn't flinch.
Her hand hovered above the chain,
and in that moment,
it wasn't just the star she was freeing—
it was herself.
She had spent so long fighting to be heard,
to be seen,
to hold onto her own light.
But now she understood: the light wasn't something you waited
for.
It was something you carried inside.

The light isn't just freed.
It is claimed.

With every breath,
    the air around her seemed to tighten.
    Her voice broke the silence—
    not with fear, not with hesitation—
    but with the full force of her heart's conviction.

    "Justice is love refusing to be silenced!"

    Her voice was thunder rolling across the mountain,
    echoing through the trees,
    through the very earth beneath her feet.
    It wasn't just sound—
    it shook the very air,
    vibrating with a force that made the ground tremble.

The sisters staggered back,
    their faces pale with shock,
    as if her words were a storm they couldn't outrun.
    Her voice split the sky.
    The mountain answered with a low rumble,
    a breath it had held for ages—
    finally released.
    It wasn't just the force of her words—
    it was the truth behind them,
    carrying the weight of generations.
    Her voice didn't just fill the air—
    it flooded it,
    dissolving the silence that had held the world still for so long.
    She looked at the star,

knowing it had always been hers to set free.
She didn't have to be chosen.
She was already the one who could do it.
And she wasn't going to let the pain of others keep her in the
dark anymore.

"You don't get to hold the light hostage just because it didn't save
you," she said

in her thunderous voice,
her voice full of power,
full of the realization that the moment had come.
She wasn't just fighting for the star.
She was fighting for everything the star represented:
truth, love, and the courage to stand in the face of despair.
And with that, she touched the chain.

Chapter Nine: The Unchaining

The moment Myla's fingers touched the chain,
    a jolt—
    pure lightning—
    surged through her.
    Not fire,
    but something ancient
    stirring from a long, bitter sleep.
    The star surged beneath the bindings-
    sensing her touch.
    Aurelia flinched.

Eris took a step back.
But Myla didn't stop.
She placed both hands on the chain.
It burned.
Not on her skin—
her soul.

Images flashed through her—memories not her own.
    Wishes carried to the star across lifetimes.
    Some pure.
    Some selfish.
    Some broken beyond recognition.
    The star had carried them all.
    That was its burden.
    And its purpose.

The chain was not made of metal.
    It was made of grief.
    Each link forged from promises that were never kept,
    from people who wished
    but walked away,
    from hearts that asked for light,
    then rejected it when it required change.
    The sisters had only wrapped the final binding.
    But the chain?
    We had all helped build it.
    Myla understood then—
    this wasn't just about her.
    It wasn't even just about the sisters.
    This was about everyone.
    Everyone who had ever wished for a better world,
    but refused to become it.

Everyone who wanted miracles
but not the transformation that came with them.
Everyone who had once believed–
then stopped.
Because it's never what it seems.
The wish doesn't arrive as you imagine.
It comes disguised—
as hardship,
as silence,
as trial.
It prepares you without telling you why.
And by the time it reveals itself,
you've already become the one who can carry it.

Myla understood now—
    The wish hadn't been just the star.
    It had been the mountain, too.
    The journey and the destination.
    The pain that refined her,
    and the light that remembered her.
    Even the villagers who had shunned her—
    they had unknowingly answered the wish.
    Because without their exile,
    she might never have answered the call,
    the call to find the truth of who she was.

And now, the star was fading.
    Not because it had no power.
    But because it had no one left to believe in it.
    Myla's tears fell—not from pain,
    but from the weight of it all.

                          .   .   .

"I won't walk away," her voice steady and soft.
    "I won't leave you behind."
    The star thrummed.
    Brighter.
    Alive.

As her hands pressed harder into the chain,
    Myla sensed something change.
    A warmth spread from her palms,
    and she saw it—
    the hands of her ancestors,
    transparent and glowing,
    layered over her own.
    The strength of generations rose inside her,
    and she surrendered—
    to the moment,
    to the current,
    to the ones who had never left her.
    Her grandmother.
    Her father, Jax.
    All the souls who had come before her—
    guiding her hands,
    lending their power.

The storm surged.
    Electricity crackled in the air.
    Wind howled around her,
    the whispering fury of a thousand voices,
    but Myla did not falter.
    She held the chain,
    feeling the weight of her family's sacrifices,
    feeling the power of her ancestors' light coursing through her.

· · ·

"Stop!" Aurelia screamed,
    her voice seething with rage, mingling with the wind.
    "You don't understand!
    This is selfish!
    You only wanted the star for yourself!"
    Eris' voice joined in,
    more desperate,
    almost pleading:
    "Do you think you can bear this burden?
    Do you think you're worthy?
    You're a fool, Myla.
    A fool who thinks you can change the fate of the stars?"

But Myla didn't stop.
    She heard their words.
    But they no longer had power over her.
    She was not alone.
    Her ancestors were with her,
    and so was the star.
    She pressed harder into the chain.
    Her hands burned,
    yet the power of a thousand lifetimes steadied her grip.
    The storm raged around her—
    a whirl of wind,
    lightning, and energy—but it no longer terrified her.
    She had become the storm.
    And as the storm reached its peak,
    The spiral universe locket began to glow.
    the necklace chain began to crack—
    slowly at first,
    then faster,

as the final link shattered in a burst of light
and sound.
The storm exploded into a flash of blinding light,
the air vibrating with energy,
and for a moment,
Myla thought she might be swept away.
But her hands remained steady.
The chain that held the star cracked.
Not all at once.
It unraveled, a spell in reverse—
a thousand quiet lies dissolving in the presence of one single
truth.

Myla said, "I still believe."

The light returned—first soft,
then rising.
The chains fell into dust.
Aurelia screamed.
Eris covered her face.
The mountain shuddered.
And the star—
the star began to burn.
Not with fire.
With truth.
It rose higher,
no longer chained,
no longer crying.
And Myla—
Myla stood in its glow,
arms open,
eyes wide,
her chest filled with something she hadn't felt in a long time.
Peace.

Chapter Ten : The Rise of the Love Warrior

The star burned brighter now—
    no longer flickering,
    no longer bound.
    It hovered above the summit,
    pulsing with light that wasn't fire,
    wasn't flame—
    It was remembrance.

The star hovered above the summit,

pulsing with a light that was no longer fire—
no longer flame—
but something older.
Something remembered.
Myla felt it.
Not words.
Not sound.
But knowing.
The star was speaking.
Not aloud,
but into her thought and memory
braided with light:

I feel... I've returned from the edge of forgetting.
For so long,
I drifted in silence—
dimmed not by time,
but by disbelief.
Not rage.
Not bitterness.
Just... absence.
Not because I wasn't visible.
But because I was no longer seen for what I truly was.
I wasn't forgotten all at once—
but slowly,
as hearts stopped believing,
as eyes turned away from wonder.
I was not seen,
so I began to disappear.
But you—
you looked up.
Even when the world gave you every reason not to.
Even when you were broken, you believed.
And belief—true belief—reverberates across worlds.

You called me back.
I don't shine like I once did.
I shine in a new way now—
brighter, deeper, older.
Not fire. Not flame.
But remembrance of who we are beneath the forgetting.
Of what still shines when everything else fades.
You didn't just save me, Myla.
You reminded me that hope is never extinct—
only waiting.
Waiting for one soul to remember.
And now,
as I hover above the summit,
I don't look down on the world.
I reach for it.
Because if even one can believe...
perhaps others will too.
I was once a star.
But now...
I am the mirror of your courage
And I shine because you do.

The star was shining a light that doesn't just illuminate...
but restores.
The light found what was broken,
and gathered it back.
Not to make it what it was—
but it made it whole in a new way.
The kind of light that touches the forgotten,
the fractured,
the fading—
and says:
You still belong to the sky.

. . .

Myla turned her gaze away from the star—
and saw her.
Not the enchantress cloaked in beauty,
but the truth beneath it.
The threads of deception unraveling,
the hunger behind the hollow deception.
Light doesn't lie.
And in its presence,
neither could she.
Aurelia stumbled back,
shielding her face.
Her shimmering gown had begun to dull,
threads unraveling as if the light itself refused to reflect off her
lies.
Eris collapsed to her knees.
Not in pain—but in shock.
Her mouth trembling.

Myla stood at the center of it all.
Bathed in the star's glow.
Silent.
Steady.
At that moment... the mountain stirred.
Not to celebrate.
Not to speak.
But because it, too,
had reached its moment.
It had carried her in silence—
not as a throne,
but as a guardian.
A witness.
A father made of stone.
It had thrummed when she was in danger.

It had steadied her when she chose truth.
And now,
It received her—
not to lift her,
but to meet her.
Two halves of the same force.
One who held.
One who rose.

She looked up at the star.
    And the star... looked back.
    For the first time, she saw it clearly.
    It wasn't just a star.

    It was a soul.

    A soul made of every selfless wish ever whispered,
    every sacrifice no one saw,
    every child who loved with their whole heart
    and never asked for anything in return.
    It was the soul of the universe,
    and she was a part of it.
    She always had been.

Slowly—
    The star began to descend.
    Not with weight.
    But with intimacy.
    It came to her level,
    hovered before her,
    radiant with images.
    Memories.

Moments.
Not from the world...
From her.

The memory of when she heard the star for the first time—
    and knew she had never truly been alone.
    The moment she believed.
    The moment Wolf tried to break her—
    The moment the mountain stood with her.
    The first time she had been shunned.
    The moment Jeval tried to twist her truth—
    and she remembered who she was.
    The night she looked up at the stars with tears on her face
    and spoke, *Please let there be more.*
    The moment she forgot.
    The moment she remembered again.
    And the star spoke—
    not in sound,
    but in soul:

You are ready.

Myla didn't respond.
She didn't need to.
Her whole being answered.
Myla stood still,
    her hand pressed gently against her chest,
    where the spiral galaxy locket had once rested,
    warm and constant.
But there was nothing there.
The locket had vanished—
    The fire that had consumed the necklace on the summit, leaving
only an empty space where a piece of her past had been.

A sense of loss washed over her.
A fleeting ache,
a twinge of grief.
The locket had been a gift from her Abuela,
a symbol of guidance
and connection to the universe.
It had been her anchor,
reminding her of the journey she had to take
and the truth she needed to remember.
But now—
no locket.
Myla's fingers brushed over her chest again,
half—expecting the cool metal to be there.
Her thoughts drifted back to Abuela's words:

This is not just a galaxy. It's a map. A reminder.

In the stillness of the moment,
with the wind whispering through the trees,
something inside her awoke.
She remembered what her Abuela had once told her—

You carry the whole universe inside you.

Back then, she couldn't believe it.
    She wanted to.
    But part of her still needed proof.
    The locket had been that proof.
    But now it was gone.
    And in the space where certainty use to live,
    Something softer entered.
    she embodied the truth

she knew she didn't need the locket.
She never did.
The map had always been within her.
The universe had never been outside of her.
It was inside her—
woven into her soul—
threads of light that had always existed,
waiting to be recognized.
Her chest eased;
the absence of the locket no longer carried the weight of loss.
It was a realization—
a truth that she had been carrying within her all along.
She no longer needed a physical reminder of her connection to the stars.
She was the map. She was the universe,
its light and its darkness,
its wisdom and its mystery.
Everything that had once seemed outside her was now a part of her—
intertwined in the very essence of her being.
Her heart fluttered as the realization settled in,
a soft light growing stronger within.
She was the love warrior the star had called for.
No locket was needed to tell her that.
The star pulsed in reply.

At last—
It began to dissolve.
Not in destruction.
In becoming.
It flowed into the mountain,
into the sky,
into the wind,

into Myla.
Into everything.
And for a moment—
all of it was white light.
Not blinding,
but whole.
The mountain pulsed with it.
The sky breathed with it.
Myla's heart glowed with it.
And all the pieces of her journey—
the fire,
the sorrow,
the stars,
even the silence—
were part of it now.
It flowed into the mountain,
into the sky,
into the wind,
Into the earth.

And beneath it all—
a river beneath silence—
was the current.
The current she had always felt but never named.
Now she knew:
it had carried her all along.
She hadn't just freed the star.
She had walked through a constellation doorway—
and stepped into the miracle she was always meant to become.
Because now, the light no longer needed to stand alone.
The star had found its love warrior

. . .

Out of the corner of her eye she saw Aurelia stripped of glamour,
  looked at her hands as if seeing them for the first time.
  Eris wept–
  but no longer from bitterness.
  From recognition.

Myla stood firm,
  her feet grounded by the weight of the mountain beneath her,
  while the sky above opened wide—
  Vast, infinite, eternal.
  She felt the energy of Aurelia's gaze–
  those cracks in her resolve,
  the sorrow clinging to her like a shadow.
  It wasn't anger that Myla saw in Aurelia's eyes,
  but the weight of all that she had surrendered:
  the light, the hope, the love.
  The very things that Myla had fought to hold onto.

Eris remained in the background,
  a distant figure, a witness to the truth Myla was finally seeing.
  The real battle,
  however,
  wasn't between Eris and Myla.
  It was between Myla and Aurelia—
  the one who had once held the light
  but let it slip away,
  and the one who had found it again.
  "I see you,"
   Myla said softly,
  her voice carrying not only through the space between them
  but through the very fabric of the universe.

"But I won't walk the path you walked.
    I won't let the darkness swallow me like it did you.

In this moment of recognition,
Myla understood.
Aurelia's surrender hadn't come from cruelty–
But from brokenness.
From the unbearable weight of trying to be everything
For everyone
and nothing for herself.
It was the same choice Myla had once faced:
To give in,
Or to rise.
She chose to rise.
She chose to rise because she had seen the light—
despite all the shadow that had tried to smother it.
It was etched in her memory and into her soul.
She rose because she realized
The true battle was never outside her–
but within.
She rose because the light inside her
was worth the fight.
This moment–the choice—
was where the light would be reborn.

Aurelia stepped back.
    Her image was fading.
    Not shattered–
    But undone.
    She turned,
    Not defeated,
    But released.
    Aurelia's shell of perfection

began to crack—
The sheen of protection she wore—
Her polished armor of charm and control—
shattered under the light of the star.
And then her face softened.
The mask she had crafted so carefully
melted— not from heat,
But from truth.
And beneath it,
Myla saw someone scared.
Not dangerous.
Just tired.
Just lost.

Eris stood behind her,
    Silent
    Watching.
    Her hands were shaking,
    But her eyes were no longer
    hard.
    Tears fell freely—
    not from bitterness
    but from recognition.
    She didn't speak.
    She didn't argue.
    She simply stepped forward
    And placed a hand gently on
    Aurelia's back.

Together, they turned.
    Not defeated.
    But undone.

Whether they would rise again,
She did not know.
But they would no longer
Guard the summit.
Not now.
Not ever again.
With their final steps,
the weight lifted.
Their forms thinned as they walked
And they dissolved into the night.

Then, the sky broke open in light.
Not blinding.
Welcoming.
And as Myla stood at the top of the mountain,
alone—
and not alone,
she closed her eyes for a moment.
The wind touched her cheek,
a memory in motion.
She thought of the girl she once was—
who gazed at the stars,
unsure,
lost,
and full of longing.
But now,
she stood as a Love Warrior,
her heart alight with purpose.

She had made a wish once.
For someone to see her.
To understand her.

To tell her she didn't have to change to be worthy of love.
And she found it–
in the most unexpected place.
Not in a star.
Not in another.
But in herself.
She said to herself,

"I am the light of love."

She was the one she had been waiting for all along,
The light.
The love.
And in that knowing,
a voice rose from within:

"I see you. I choose you."

she surrendered to the light—
to the truth she'd carried all along.
She had remembered her true self–
The one who broke the cycle and the silence.
And in the moment she set something ancient free.

And maybe that's why you're here: to remember too.

Because the story didn't end with her.
The star had passed its light forward—
into the sky,
into the world,
into the hearts of those who still dare to believe.
And so she whispered to the wind, to the stars, and to you:
"Let the wishes begin—with you."

EPILOGUE

The Light That Remains

The mountain faded into memory.
    The star no longer hovered above it—
    because it had returned to where it had always belonged:

In us.

    In those who keep climbing,
    even when the path vanishes.
    In those who believe,
    even after belief feels foolish.
    In those who love,
    even after the world tries to convince them not to.

. . .

Myla stayed at the summit for a while.
 She sat in reverence beneath the sky,
 And then she stood–
 And began her descent.
 The trees bowed gently as she passed.
 The wind seemed to hum her name.
 She did not rush.
 She moved slowly down the winding paths,
 Resting beneath trees,
 Drinking from cool springs,
 She didn't need to speak.
 Father mountain had already heard her.
 She didn't descend the
 Mountain in triumph.
 She descended slowly–
 Quietly–
 wearing something new.
 Not a robe.
 Not a crown.
 But something felt.

It took her days.
 And with each step down,
 The current within her deepened–
 A steady hum, a soft knowing
 The kind that doesn't speak, but *remembers*.
 On the third night,
 As she neared the forest's edge,
 She looked up and saw it.

A new star.

Not blazing.

Not proud.

But present.

It was not the same star she had freed.

It was the one that rises in each of us when we remember who
we are.

The path was the same.

But she was not.

And as her feet touched the earth of the village once more,

She didn't speak of the summit.

She didn't have to.

Something in her presence moved through the air–

Subtle, but unmistakable.

People paused without knowing why.

Something in her stillness carried weight.

Her smile stirred remembrance.

They could not name it.

Only feel it.

They were drawn to her by something older than thought.

A frequency their hearts remembered,

even if their minds did not.

Like a melody forgotten,

Playing far off–

Just loud enough to stir

Something deep.

They didn't understand what had changed,

Only it had.

And that somehow,

they needed her now.

And though the star had returned to the sky,

its light remained—

in the hearts of those who still remembered.

Myla did not climb another mountain.

She stayed.
She found a small clearing near the edge of the woods.
There, she built a hearth—
not of stone or fire alone, but of love.
A place where travelers could rest.
Where love was served, and warriors rose.

Where those who had been cast out could be seen.
Where quiet ones could speak without fear.
She called it: The Love Warrior Hearth.

And when people asked why she made it,
she only smiled and said,
"Because someone once did the same for me."
She moved among them—not apart,
but gently,
But with quiet patience
Sowing seeds meant to bloom in a time beyond her own.
In time... they would come.
One by one.
With wishes tucked in their palms.
With sorrow pressed behind their eyes.
With hands outstretched, asking:
"Can the star still hear me?"
And Myla would smile.
Not as a prophet.
But as a girl who once believed in the sky when no one else did.
And she would say:
"Yes. It always has."

Because the stars have been waiting for someone to remember

that we are all connected.
That every wish,
every soul,
every sacrifice is shared.
That light cannot be owned–
only honored.
Because when one soul awakens,
it lights the way for the rest.
All you have to do is believe.
And the current will meet you.
And when we rise,
we rise together.
The End.
And also—
The Beginning...

AFTERWORD

A Message from the Other Side of the Veil
To the One Who's Starting to Remember

This story began not on paper, but in the space between worlds.

Years ago, I had a near—death experience — an unraveling of all I thought I knew, and a remembering of everything I had forgotten.

In that moment, I wasn't afraid. I was surrounded by a vast, shimmering stillness... and I understood, without words, that we are not just bodies moving through time. We are stars. We are souls. We are part of something ancient, infinite, and full of love.

I saw that the stars above us are not just burning balls of gas — They are beings. Souls. Lives waiting to be lived. They are ancestors. They are the unborn. They are wishes yet to be answered.

And I knew, without question, that everything we do, every act of courage, every whisper of love, every step toward truth — it echoes. It sends ripples through the sky like waves of light, connecting us across lifetimes.

The Warrior and the Star is the story that came through me in the years that followed. It was whispered by something greater.

Guided by the love of those I've lost — and those I've yet to meet. It's the journey of a soul, a child, a seeker... and it's yours, too.

This book is for the ones who have loved deeply.

For the ones who have lost.

For the ones who remember what it feels like to be home among the stars.

May it help you remember.

I didn't write this story for everyone.

I wrote it for the one who needed it.

For the one who's been silenced.

The one who almost gave up.

The one climbing through something no one else sees.

Writing this story helped me survive.

It healed something in me I didn't know could be healed.

Maybe, somehow, it will help you too.

Everything you're going through is preparing you for something sacred.

Even when it doesn't feel like it.

Especially when it doesn't feel like it.

Keep going.

I didn't know it at the time,

but the moment I began telling the truth—

not just out loud, but to myself—

everything began to change.

Because that's what truth does.

It doesn't just set you free.

It shows you the gift you've carried all along.

And once you see it—really see it—

you know exactly what you're meant to give the world.

This story is my offering.

all of it began with truth.

What if we all did that?

What if we each faced our truth,

uncovered our gift,

and gave it freely?
Maybe that's how we change everything.
One truth at a time.
One soul at a time.
Your light matters.
The star is waiting.

Wishes Are Vows:
The Soul's Contract With the Universe

A wish is not just a hope.
  It is a contract between the soul and the universe.
  To wish is to whisper a sacred promise:
  "If this is meant for me, I will rise to meet it."
  We do not simply receive miracles.
  We become them.
  And with every miracle comes a responsibility—
  To hold it with grace.
  To honor it with action.
  To protect it with truth.
  To wish is to vow.
  To do the work.
  To walk the path.
  To carry the light.
  Because wishes are not made to be granted.
  They are made to awaken us.
  And when the universe answers,
  it doesn't hand us the gift.
  It hands us the opportunity to become
  the version of ourselves
  who is ready to receive it.
  So be careful what you wish for—
  Not because it won't come true...
  but because it might.
  And when it does,
  it will change everything.

The Love Warrior

(Born of the Star, Forged on the Mountain)
I did not become this in a moment.
I became this on a mountain.
Step by trembling step.
Truth by broken truth.
Trial by trial.
Loss by loss.
I was not chosen.
I chose.
I walked through doubt, through silence,
through voices that told me to go back,
to be smaller, quieter, and to stay invisible and call it safety.
But I remembered—
not with my mind,
with my soul.
The wish. The light. The vow.
They tried to call it a burden.
But it was always sacred.
A Love Warrior is not born in comfort.
She is born in the silence after betrayal.
In the rising after collapse.
In the moment she finally says:
No more.
No more self—abandonment.
No more shrinking.
No more betraying the truth
for the illusion of peace.
She does not fight with rage.
She fights with love sharpened by clarity.
She fights with truth that does not blink.

She carries the names of the ones she loves like stars inside her
ribs.
And she knows—
she remembers—
she is not alone.
She is part of a constellation.
A current.
A lineage of those who rose
when the world said, "You can't."
She stands united with them—
she is their echo.
Their answer.
The wish they once whispered into the dark.
And now—
I make my own vow:
I will not let you harm me.
I will not let you harm the ones I love.
And I will never again harm myself
for someone else's comfort.
I do not stand here flawless.
I stand here forged.
I am not the end of the story.
I am the beginning of the light.
I am a Love Warrior.
And I remember the star.
Because it lives in me now.

—Myla

ACKNOWLEDGMENTS

For Jax,
> who stepped in when no one else did.
> You saw the places that hurt,
> and loved them whole.
> Even now, you are.
> Your love healed something I thought was unhealable.
> And the gift you left me—
> wasn't just this story.
> It was the strength to live it.

For my Abuela,
> the origin of my love—
> and the first Love Warrior.
> Everything I know of tenderness,
> of devotion, of strength wrapped in softness—
> came from her.
> The love I give to Wyatt,
> the love I pour into these pages,
> the love I carry in every breath—
> is hers, echoing through me
> And every brave thing I've done
> began with her.

For my mother,
> whose soul I chose,

and who chose mine—
so we could walk the path
of transformation together.
Through her love, in all its forms,
I was given the lessons I needed
to evolve,
to remember,
to rise.

For Melanie,
    Who stood by when the path was uncertain,
    and whose presence reminded me
    that I didn't have to walk it alone.

For Curtis,
    Who stood in quiet strength,
    and protected what was sacred.

For Sage, my lantern in the dark.
    You held the light steady while I remembered it was mine.
    The one who rose from the ashes with quiet strength,
    whose light reached me when I couldn't find my own.

And most of all—
    To the Current that carried me,
    answered my prayer,
    and carried me when I could not walk.
    And to the one I became when I remembered.
    Thank you for surviving.
    Thank you for choosing love.

ABOUT THE AUTHOR

Margot Michelle Eaton is a storyteller, therapist, and mother who believes in the quiet power of presence, truth, and remembering who we are beneath the noise.

She has spent over two decades in healing spaces—not to fix or lead, but to sit beside others with open hands and an open heart.

Her work is rooted in quiet service—never to fix, but to witness, to honor, and to walk beside others as they remember their own light.

She believes stories are a kind of soul medicine—gently helping us return to ourselves.

The Warrior and the Star is her first novel—
written first as a lantern for her son,
a soul bright boy whose heart lights every room,
for anyone still searching for that same light in themselves.
For the quiet ones. The kind ones.
The ones who carry what no one sees.
The ones who've lost more than they let on—
and still found a way to love.
But most of all,
this is for those who no longer know what to believe—
and long, somewhere deep inside,
to remember that magic is real.
That they matter.
That they were never alone.

She lives in California, where she continues to write, teach, and honor the ones still gathering the courage to climb.

Contact:
Thewarriorandthestar.com
Thewarriorandthestar@gmail.com